The Angry Gymnast

The Angry Gymnast

by

Jerry B. Jenkins

MOODY PRESS
CHICAGO

ISBN: 0-8024-8235-X

5   6   Printing/LC/Year   90   89   88

Printed in the United States of America

To Sandy Picklesimer Aldrich

Contents

1

Meeting a True Superstar

I had talked with Deborah Lambert on the phone, but I had never met her. She was the one who had called to see if she could join the Baker Street Sports Club.

That had been back when we had got so much newspaper coverage about our baseball and basketball teams. She was new in my church, interested in all major sports, and not aware that the Baker Street Sports Club was for boys only.

There had been mixed reactions from the guys when I first told them about her. Some said no way, no girls in the club. Others thought it would be OK if she was a good athlete and cute, or either.

The sport in question at that time was football, and even though I had read about a few high school girls who had played football with the boys' team, we weren't ready for that.

When I called Deborah back, I used the excuse that she was too old. "We do have an age limit. Twelve." I heard the chuckle from the other end of the line.

"Oh, my, I am too old! Ancient compared to that. And isn't that the story of my life."

It was more of a statement than a question, and I didn't know what she meant by that, but she was pleasant about it and seemed real nice for an older girl. I guessed she was about seventeen, but I was wrong. Not by much, but by enough, which makes a difference, as you'll see.

Deborah had told me she had first heard about me in church and then read about our club in the paper. For several Sundays after that, I kept asking my mother to point her out to me. But my mother wasn't sure which one she was either.

"I know she was some sort of an olympian, though, Dallas. Someone told me that."

Finally, the day came when she and her family joined the church and were introduced at the front. I realized I had seen her many times before, without knowing who she was. Deborah was tall and lithe with short hair and perfect, smooth skin. I thought she was a knockout, but I didn't risk telling anyone else that.

When our pastor introduced the family, he referred to her as "an alternate on the U.S. olympic gymnastics team." That got my attention. She had said she specialized in gymnastics, but this was something else. She wasn't all tight and muscly like a lot of women gymnasts, but she moved just as gracefully.

On Sunday night a week later, I was sitting in church with my parents and my two little sisters when I felt hands on my shoulders just before the service began. I didn't know which way to turn, and I didn't know who it was, so I didn't move.

Someone whispered in my right ear. "So, when are you going to let me coach the Baker Street Sports Club in some sport?" I knew it was Deborah Lambert, even though I was too nervous and embarrassed to turn and look at her.

"What would you coach?"

"Volleyball, tennis, basketball—I've played them all."

"But you're a gymnast, right?"

"Yeah, but I don't suppose you guys have a gymnastics team."

I felt silly sitting there whispering to a girl who was sitting behind me. "Stranger things have happened. We might start one if we had the right coach. I couldn't dream of a better

4

choice."

"But you don't just up and start a team when you've had no experience."

"Oh, yes, we do. We did in swimming and hockey. In fact, we've done that in lots of sports."

The organ began playing. She patted my shoulders and said we could talk about it after church.

You know, I really liked the way she talked to me. It made me feel special. I mean, who would expect an olympic athlete to talk to a kid anyway? It wasn't that I was interested in her or anything. I was still sort of anti-girls, but I have to admit I looked forward to seeing her after church.

In fact, I sort of had trouble concentrating on the songs and the sermon, and for some reason, I was more worried about standing around talking to a girl than I was about what we were going to talk about.

Most of the people I talked to were boys my age and sometimes their parents. If I talked to girls my age, I was usually teasing them or trying to convince them that I didn't want to talk with them. That's what most of my friends did too, even though we had our favorites, ones we thought were cute or liked us.

Well, after the service, I found out how much of a take-charge person Deborah Lambert was. I started to file out with my family, expecting that she and I would connect in the foyer somewhere, but she just sat on the back of my pew and started talking.

My dad pointed to his watch, and the rest of them headed for the car. I nodded, but I wasn't sure how long I'd be. It's hard to explain how I felt standing there talking to this beautiful, world-class athlete.

I was embarrassed, and yet I liked it. I knew people saw me with her and had to be wondering what we were talking about. I wasn't very good at upholding my end of the conversation, so I was glad she seemed confident and talked a lot.

"If you and your friends are serious about possibly starting

5

a gymnastics team, you might want to look into it down at the North American Turner Gym."

"Never heard of it."

"Most people haven't. It takes its name from the old-fashioned word for gymnasts and tumblers: 'turners.' No one who comes to that gym is there to play or to show off or hop around in an aerobics class. The only type of person we get is the serious gymnast. We run the others off."

"But my friends and I wouldn't be serious gymnasts. We'd be beginners."

"Oh, you can be both. And you'd better be, or I wouldn't want to coach you."

I scratched my head, not because it itched but because it was my turn to talk and I didn't know what to say. "Are you telling me that you really would coach a little gymnastics team if the Baker Street Sports Club put one together?"

She smiled. "I'd love to."

"We can't pay you, and I don't know where we'd train."

"I don't want money, Dallas. I want to be involved with the types of boys you have in your club. I've heard and read a lot about you, and I want to help you, that's all. If I could have been in a club like yours when I was a kid, well—"

"But where would we find equipment or, uh—"

"Apparatus?"

I nodded.

"At the North American Turner Gym. I work there and train there. There would be a small fee for using the apparatus, but from what I know about your club, you can raise the money for uniforms and have plenty left over for that."

"What would we do before we get our uniforms?"

"You can rent outfits at the gym. Very reasonable."

I shook my head. She had thought of everything. "I'd better get going out to the car, Deborah." I started moving that direction. She walked with me. "Sometime could you tell me about being in the olympics?"

I thought I saw her face cloud over. "I was just an alternate,

6

you know. I didn't compete."

"Yeah, but you went, didn't you? I mean, you traveled internationally, and you had to be there in uniform in the parade and everything, just in case someone got hurt."

She nodded. "It was something."

"Can you tell me about it sometime?"

"There's not much to tell."

Something was wrong; that was clear. I didn't know where to go with the conversation, and we were nearing the pastor.

"You two finding some sports types of things to talk about?"

I nodded and smiled.

Deborah was more open. She shook his hand. "We sure are."

Suddenly, we were outside in the crisp air. "Listen, Dallas, you come to the gym tomorrow night after dinner, you and any of your friends you want to bring and who you know will behave themselves. I'll arrange for Stan, our equipment manager, to get you outfitted so you won't feel out of place and can get familiar with some of the apparatus. And as soon as I've finished with my junior girls and my own half-hour workout, I'll walk you through the mens' events. Fair enough?"

I nodded. "Yeah. Except one thing."

"Anything."

"Are you sure?"

"About what?"

"That I can ask you anything."

"Well, sure, I can't imagine anything a nice young Christian boy would ask me that I wouldn't answer."

"I was just wondering if you were training for the next olympics."

There was a long silence, and I knew I had upset her. I hadn't meant to do that. My dad and mom and sisters were in one of the few cars left in the parking lot, but they weren't honking or anything. I stared at her. I wanted an answer. She had not wanted to talk about the olympics before, and now the idea of the next olympics had made her quiet too.

"You realize we just had the olympics, Dallas."

"Yeah, so there's another one in what—a little over three years? You were an alternate, so you'll be on the team next time, right? I mean, that makes sense, doesn't it?"

She nodded. "Well, you see that's a problem for me. I'm nineteen years old, almost twenty."

"So?"

"So, my time is past."

"At twenty?!"

"I'm afraid so. I was the second to the oldest girl who went to the olympic games earlier this year, and several that I narrowly edged out were fourteen and fifteen."

"So, they'll be—"

"Eighteen and nineteen by the next olympics. And they will be the old lady alternates, most likely. It's the girls who are twelve now, the ones we've never seen, never competed with, who will be our first team then."

"And you'll be what, a twenty-three-year-old olympic coach by then?"

She laughed. "No. But you see, Dallas, there's a reason this is so painful for me. Do you have time to hear it?"

I looked at my parents' car and wished I hadn't. They were waiting with the engine running. "I'd really love to, but—"

"That's all right. I'd rather not talk about it anyway."

"No! I really do want to know."

"Well, then you come early tomorrow evening, by yourself, and I'll tell you."

2

The North American Turner Gym

I arranged for Jack, Toby, Jimmy, Bugsy, Brent, and Ryan to come to the gym early the next evening. Meanwhile, I went right after dinner so I would be sure to get a chance to talk with Deborah Lambert before everyone else got there.

There was hardly anyone at the gym when I got there. Stan, the equipment man, told me that this was the slow hour of the day. "It's when the coaches and instructors either work out on their own or go out for dinner."

I wondered aloud whether Miss Lambert was in. He wasn't sure, but he didn't think so. "She tol' me you were comin' and asked me to get you outfitted. What size are ya?"

A few minutes later I was wearing an all-white uniform with gymnastics slippers, stretch pants with stirrups and shoulder straps, and a shirt. He tossed me a dark green towel and asked me what I had in my duffel bag.

"Just my Baker Street Sports Club jacket."

"Lemme see it."

I showed him the blue jacket with the red, white, and blue piping that all the guys in our club wear for every sport except football (the jackets don't fit over our shoulder pads). "I didn't know if it was right for gymnastics or not, Mr., uh—"

"Stan. Just call me Stan. Yeah, it'll work. And you may need it. It gets pretty hot in this gym when you're workin' out, but then we turn on the vent or open a window or two when it gets stuffy, and everybody likes to have a jacket or a sweater or somethin' so their muscles don't tighten up on 'em."

I nodded and dug out the jacket. I laid the towel across my arm and stuffed my street clothes into the duffel bag. On the way across the men's gym to the locker room, Stan said that he would show me all the men's apparatus, " 'cept Deborah threatened me to within an inch of my life if I tol' you anything she wants to tell you. So you can just look at the stuff on your way, and she'll tell ya about it when she gets back."

"You're sure she's not here?"

"Not dead sure, no. I didn't see her leave, I mean, but I was in the back. If she's here, she's either in the coaches' lounge, the women's locker room, or the women's gym. You're free to look around, 'slong as you stay out of the lounge and the women's locker room."

There were so few people working out that the gym seemed to echo. One guy, about five-feet-ten and a hundred eighty pounds, ran from one end of the floor to about the middle at top speed. There was no floor exercise mat or anything on the hardwood, so I had no idea what he was going to do besides run.

When he reached the middle of the floor, he leaped straight out, headfirst, almost as if he was going to slide into a base, but he was about four feet off the ground. No way he could land on his belly on the hard floor at that speed.

Just as he began to come down, he dropped his palms flat on the floor and tucked his head under. His hands stuck on the floor, and his speed and momentum brought his hips and legs over the top. As he did his top speed somersault, his feet landed lightly, and he stopped in what appeared to be a floor exercise pose. If he was aware anyone else was in the room, it wasn't apparent.

His red face and shoulders showed the strain of the exercise,

12

but he quickly leaped to his feet, jogged back to his starting point, and ran through it again. As light and delicate as he made the maneuver look, the closer I got, the louder were the hard thuds against the ground as his shoulders and hips and heels hit.

The only other gymnast in the place was standing beneath the still rings, two parallel wood circles suspended from the ceiling by straps. For the longest time, he seemed to just stare at the rings. They were high above his head, and it appeared that he could just reach them if he leaped from the floor, which, presently, he did.

He caught a ring in each hand and hung with his arms fully extended until the rings stopped swinging. That looked easy enough, but then I had never tried it. Slowly, he pulled his feet up and over his head, doing a backward flip and letting go of the rings at the end of the turn.

He landed neatly on his feet, stood staring at the rings until they settled again, jumped and hung from them, and started the same process again. Just as I was about to head to a smaller gym across the hall, he leaped again, but this time the routine was different.

Rather than pulling his legs up over his head, he forced his hands down to his waist and suspended himself vertically. Then he let his hands go straight out to his sides. He made it look easy until I saw the strain in his arms and in his face.

His cheeks bulged, his eyes squinted, his arms shook. It was then I realized some of what gymnastics was all about. The competition I had seen on television made it all look so fun and easy, and when you saw the men olympians interviewed, it was easy to think that their big muscles made the exercises simple for them.

But there in the gym it was a different story. That rings man was obviously a talented gymnast, strong and well-trained. Yet the effort that went into making a difficult task look easy was incredible.

His entire body weight was supported by his arms, and

they were straight out to the sides. When he could stand it no longer, he let his body descend slowly, his hands and arms above his head. Then, he did his back flip dismount again and sat with his back against the wall, breathing heavily. I wondered if he thought it was fun in spite of all the work.

Just after the floor exercise man hit his hard somersault one more time, I turned away. The women's gym was dark except for the eerie lights from the exit signs. I stepped into the room and immediately found myself on a one-inch rubberized mat.

As my eyes adjusted to the darkness, I could see it was the floor exercise mat. From the other end of the room I heard a squeaking noise every few seconds, unlike anything I had ever heard before.

Next to the floor ex mat was a long runway that led to a vault, the type of apparatus I had seen the olympians leap over during competition. In the middle of the floor were the uneven parallel bars, probably the silliest looking things in all of sports.

Unlike the men's parallel bars, which were even in height and on which the men swing and balance and exercise parallel to and between the bars, the women's uneven bars are just what the name implies. Uneven.

One of the bars is so much lower than the other that the girls can't exercise on it parallel to the bars. If they put one hand on one bar and the other on the other, they would be so tilted they wouldn't be able to move.

So, they attack it from the side instead of the end. I had seen tapes of the tiny Russian Olga Korbut and the Romanian Nadia Comaneci do things on the women's uneven bars that were hard to believe. They swung so fast and hit the lower bar so hard with their hips and abdomens that you just had to know they had deep bruises.

Yet it was that speed and danger that put those two young women at the top of the gymnastics world years ago.

I could still hear the squeaking but couldn't decide what was causing it. I moved toward the center of the room to get a

14

closer look at the uneven bars.

They were anchored into the floor through metal fasteners on steel cable. The supports were steel, but the bars themselves were made of wood. I ran my fingers along the chalky bars and tugged at them. They were tight, yet flexible at the same time.

In the middle they would give, and I had seen little girls make them bend from the weight and speed of their bodies. This was one event in which I had no interest as a participant.

The next time I heard a squeak from the other end of the room behind me, I thought I heard a sigh with it. That made me start, and from my squatting position near the uneven bars, I glanced back across my shoulder.

There was someone on the balance beam! A lengthy, four inch-wide block of wood set four feet off the ground by steel legs at each end, the balance beam was another of the women's events that looked fun and dangerous at the same time. I couldn't imagine why anyone would try it in the light of day, let alone in the dark.

As I watched, the tall young woman in a deep burgundy warm-up suit pranced to one end and pivoted on one toe. That was what had caused the squeak, the leather toe of her slipper on the wood grain.

That was something else you never hear on television. The girls seem to dance airily along the beam as if they hardly need to touch it. But when they flip and turn and jump, and you're close enough to hear it, the beam makes a lot of noise.

I was shocked that anyone would practice without someone watching, in case there was an accident or an injury, but the woman on the beam was every bit as good as anyone I had ever seen on television, olympic champions included.

As she turned again, I could see the USA on her back. It had to be Deborah. Though I could hear her heavy breathing, her occasional sighs and grunts, the squeaking of her slipper, and the pounding of her feet on the beam, I couldn't ignore the beauty and the grace of her performance.

15

She was working hard, sweating, torturing her body for the love of her sport, and from what I could see, it was paying off. She had already exercised much longer than I had ever seen anyone on television, yet just as she got to the place where she would normally dismount, she just pivoted and kept going.

It was beautiful. I wanted to applaud or say something, but I knew she didn't know I was even in there, and I certainly didn't want to startle her. I just stayed right where I was, transfixed, watching.

Finally, she finished. She didn't do any dramatic dismount, the way she would have in competition. It was probably the only thing she didn't do because of the danger of having no one there if she missed her landing.

She simply finished a rollover move and put her left hand on the beam, gliding to the floor with her feet. Just as the man on the rings in the other room had done, she backed up to the wall and slid into a sitting position. She drew her feet up under her and dropped her head between her knees.

I stood and slowly padded to within ten feet of her. She was very warm, I assumed, because of the workout, but there was something chilly about the room. Impulsively, I tossed her my towel.

She jumped a little as it draped neatly over her head. She pulled at it with one hand and mopped her face with it. "Thanks, Stan. I didn't see you come in."

3

Encounter in the Dark

Had I been Deborah Lambert and thought someone was somebody else, I would have been embarrassed and would have wanted the person to just leave and not humiliate me.

But I already knew Deborah well enough to know that she was not easily embarrassed. She would take this in stride, just as she did everything else.

"Uh, it's not Stan. It's me. Dallas."

She raised her head and laughed at herself. "Ah, Dallas! Thanks! You're going to have to get yourself a fresh towel now!"

"No problem."

"C'mon over and sit down. Good to see you."

I didn't know what to say. Did she really want me to sit next to her against the wall in the dark? She waved me over. "C'mon!"

I nervously settled down next to her. "You look good in your gymnastics outfit, Dallas. You're going to enjoy this sport."

"So do you."

"Enjoy it? Yeah, I guess I'd better after all the years and money I've invested in it."

"No, I mean you look good in your outfit too."

She laughed again. "I hate to work out with my sweats on, but it's best to stay warm." She took a deep breath and let it out, dropping her head between her knees again.

I began praying that no one, not my friends, not Stan the equipment man, no one would find us in there sitting in the dark.

Deborah wasn't concerned in the least.

I wasn't in the mood to talk much. "Shouldn't we turn on the light?"

"Nah. Just wastes energy. The electric company's and mine!" She thought that was pretty funny. I just smiled. She wasn't looking at me anyway.

"Why do you work out in the dark?"

She raised her head, rested her arms on her knees and her chin on her arms. "One of my secrets. You won't tell anyone, will you?"

"Who would I tell?"

"How should I know? You could be a Russian spy."

I got the impression that Deborah liked me a lot to tease me that way. I liked her too, but she made me nervous. It was as if I didn't feel I was really worthy to be the friend of an olympic athlete, even if it *was* flattering. I was afraid that maybe she would realize soon enough that I wasn't very impressive.

"Seriously, Dallas, it's good to work out in the dark. Especially on the beam. A lot of coaches and gymnasts will tell you it's hogwash, but it works for me."

"Why not just work out blindfolded?"

"It's not the same. You need some visual reference for your balance. I'll prove it to you. Stand up."

I stood.

She stayed where she was. "Lift your right leg and grab it behind you in you right hand."

I did it, lost my balance, and hopped around a little until I was steady again.

"Can you stand there without hopping?"

I said I thought so, hopped once more, and stood still.

"Stay that way a few seconds."

I tilted a little but stayed in the same spot. Then I was perfectly still.

She spoke again. "OK?"

I nodded.

"Now shut your eyes."

I shut them. A couple of seconds later I was hopping again. "Keep them shut while you try to regain your balance!"

I hopped into the wall, laughing and falling down next to her. "See, our brains need that vision reference. When I'm up on the beam in this low light, I can't see the beam, but I can see the exit signs and the wall. There's enough so that, while I have memorized the beam, I also have adequate visual input to keep my equilibrium."

"Sounds kinda complicated."

"That's only because I used the fifty cent words that my former coach used when he explained it to me. He's a Ph.D. in sports medicine and psychology."

"Hm."

"I can tell you're real interested."

"No, I am! It's just that I'm wondering if my friends are here yet."

"What time did you tell them to come?"

"Seven-thirty."

She pulled up her sleeve and held her watch toward the light. "We have a half an hour. What's on your mind?"

"What you said last night. That's why I came early."

She nodded, her lips pressed together, as if wishing I hadn't brought it up. She raised her head again, moved her arms, dropped her head, and hid from me again. She said nothing.

I don't know why, but I decided not to beg. I wasn't going to press her. She knew I wanted to know what was so upsetting to her about the olympics, both the recent ones and the ones coming up in three years or so. That was why I came, that was why I was sitting there. I wasn't going to say anything more.

21

Finally, she spoke. Her voice was muffled because of the position of her head. But I heard every word. "I have a problem, Dallas. And it's serious. You see, in the gym during practice I am the best all-around woman gymnast in the United States, maybe in the world. I'm not bragging, and if you get to know me better, you'll know that that's not the type of a person I am. Everyone says so. Not just me. In fact, I never say it. I'm saying it to you now, and I finally acknowledged it to my personal coach, but everyone else on the team knows it's true.

"We had frequent competition in practice, bringing in judges. I did something one day that no other gymnast anywhere has ever done. I achieved perfect tens in four events. Floor ex. Vault. Unevens. Beam. The coaches and the other team members crowded around the judges and asked them to review their scores—to not be lenient just because we were not competing against another team.

"The judges all insisted that they felt certain about their marks. What makes any ten so remarkable is that all the judges have to agree. The scores are always averages. With four judges you throw out the high and the low and average the other two. Our coaches wanted the four best independent judges to measure our performances to see where we stood in international competition."

I shook my head. "I'll bet they were happy that day."

"They were. And so was I. But I also froze."

"You froze."

"Can you imagine the pressure that put on me? They asked me to help coach the other, younger girls, the ones who would eventually beat me out for one of the top spots on the team. Then they expected me to be the team captain, the spiritual leader, the spokeswoman, the elder stateswoman, and, of course, the best gymnast too.

I looked over at her. She raised her head to see if I was still there. "I think I would have expected that of you too, Deborah. I mean, four tens—"

"Don't remind me."

"So, what happened?"

"You mean how did the best female gymnast in the known world fail to make the first team?"

I nodded.

"Well, we have the olympic trials on national television from Houston. I'm ready. Healthy. Prayed up. Feel good. We go into the competition, and I'm flat."

"What's that mean? Bad?"

"No, not bad. Just uninspired."

"But why? You felt so good and all that—"

"Slow down, pardner. I know all the reasons why I should have been the best again. I was being talked to by all sorts of marketing people for sportswear, breakfast cereals, cars, you name it. I could have set myself up for life with commercial endorsements alone. All hinged on my olympic performance, of course."

"Of course."

"Well, I failed."

I waited for more of an explanation. None came. "I don't understand."

"I don't either. I did my routines, I got my high scores, and they all fell short, some by hundredths of a point, others by tenths."

"That's it?"

"That's it."

"You didn't get hurt or fall or make some embarrassing mistake?"

"The only embarrassing mistake I made was that I didn't make the first team. The other girls did wonderfully. I was happy for them. But the most frustrating and disappointing thing about it all was that I had done so well. I was never lower than a nine point eight five on any event, never more than a point and a half from the perfection I had achieved in practice and which I had achieved in many meets before coming to the olympic tryouts."

"So, you just got beat."

"That's right."

"Was there anything you could have done differently? Or were the judges tougher than they had been that day in practice?"

"That's what haunts me. The judges were fair, and I did my routines the way I always did them. In looking at the video tapes, I might have worked harder, showed more effort, failed to make it look easy, but everything was there. Every difficult move was done, every position was right. I smiled a little less than usual, maybe because I had so much on my mind. But I could not have performed better, in my opinion."

I shook my head again. "That hurts."

"Boy, does it."

"All this other stuff was on your mind. You mean the commercials and all that?"

She nodded. "Until a person has gone through it, he simply cannot understand what is offered. I'm serious, Dallas. Two companies, within an hour of each other, promised me lifetime guaranteed contracts if I would endorse their products after winning a gold medal in the olympics. I would have been set for life two times over, and that was just the beginning."

"You didn't have any idea that type of thing was coming?"

"Oh, that's just it! Of course, I did. But I was not going to get my head turned. I was not going to let it affect me."

"But it did."

"It sure did."

"Why?"

4

Disappointment

I know I was asking unanswerable questions. I didn't understand what she was saying, and I knew she didn't much understand what had happened in her career either. Yet I had had to ask why, and there it hung in the dark women's part of the North American Turners' Gym.

Deborah Lambert struggled stiffly to her feet and walked to a glass-clock window that overlooked the neon lights in the street two floors below. She stood staring into the night, and I suddenly felt very sorry for her.

I knew she wouldn't want my pity, and my own feelings confused me. She seemed so warm, so loving, so caring, so disciplined, such a hard worker. The perfect athlete, maybe one of the best in the world.

But she had had her shot at the glory, the fame, the money, whatever she wanted. And in a sport where, if she had been an olympic gold medalist at nineteen, she would have been the oldest woman gymnast gold medalist in twelve years, she was—as she had already said—already an old woman.

Why had all the outside pressure affected her when she had decided in advance to not let it? She began talking in a low monotone, and I had to get up and step over behind her to hear her. "My personal coach, Omar Haller, had kept everyone away from me. He told me that everything I had heard and read and seen about how the deals are made and the lives are secured would be true, but that first I had to make the olympic team by winning a medal in the trials. Then I had to win a gold in the olympics themselves.

" 'Wait till the trials are over, and your marks make you all but a shoo-in for the olympic gold. Then you can talk to the promoters and the money people. But keep them patient. Don't sign any deals. Wait till you find out what every one has to offer, and then we'll tell them all that they're too low.' "

"Why would he advise that?"

She turned to look at me. I felt as if I were in a spotlight. The exit sign light and the blinking lights from the window lit up my face. But she stood with her back to those lights, so there was a kind of halo around her hair. Her face was in the shadows.

"All Omar cared about was the money. He's not a Christian. He knew I wanted to pay my parents back for all the time and money they had invested in my career. A lot of it went to him, you know. Tens of thousands of dollars a year."

I could hardly believe it, but I knew it was true from things I had read about figure skaters and other gymnasts.

"So he wanted some more of it?"

"Oh, yes, and I couldn't blame him. I mean, I wasn't as worried about the money as he was, and he was going to be my agent too. That would mean that he would make all the deals, handle all the arrangements, and get fifteen percent of all the money."

"That could have added up to a lot."

"You bet it could have. But there's nothing."

I was still a little confused. "But you said you talked to a couple of companies even before the olympic trials. Why did you do that?"

"Because Omar wasn't there. One thing you can't have is your personal coach hanging around with you once you get into the olympic trials and the olympics. It's a rule."

"But I saw Mary Lou Retton's coach at the 1984 olympics."

"Yes, but he wasn't allowed to talk to her or to be with her or coach her until it was all over. Omar followed the rules. I have to hand him that. He stayed out of my hair, out of my life, from the time I checked into the olympic training camp hotel until the trials were over."

"So you talked to the promoters alone?"

She nodded and walked back over to the wall. I thought she was going to sit down again, but instead she just did some light stretching and limbering exercises as she talked.

I followed her and leaned against the wall.

"Somehow they got our phone number. I mean, there was only one phone on our entire floor. It seemed there was always one of the younger girls on it, and sometimes two or three of them would hover around it, all trying to talk to someone's boyfriend at the same time.

"When they finally got off it and someone called for me, they were real excited. It was as if they knew what it was all about. They even told me what company he was with. At first I refused to come to the phone. I accused them of kidding. The caller was a former olympic champion, representing this footwear company.

"He called back several times, and finally I agreed to talk to him if everyone else would just leave me alone. They hid out of sight down the hall, but I'm sure they heard every word. I told him that my personal coach would be my agent and that he would be handling all such details. The superstar said he understood and appreciated that but was just calling to wish me luck and to set an appointment for when he and his people could talk to me and my people. Me and my people, can you imagine that? I have no people. Never did. Never will."

She fell silent for a moment. I found her story so fascinating that I wanted to pepper her with questions, but I just couldn't. For such an exciting turn of events in a person's life, it was certainly being told with a lot of sadness.

"I told him that even the appointment would have to be cleared with Omar, but he left a parting word. He said,

29

Aren't you curious to know what kind of ballpark we'll be talking in?' Dallas, I'm telling you the truth, I had no idea what he meant. I said, 'You mean we'll be meeting in a ballpark?' I thought he was going to die laughing.

"He said, 'No, we'll likely be meeting at a restaurant and then at our offices in Washington, but I mean what kind of financial figures we'll be talking about.' I was so embarrassed I almost didn't respond. Finally I said, 'Well, sure, I'm curious.' And he said, 'Let me just say this so I don't get myself in trouble with my people: at least six figures a year for the rest of your life.' "

"Six figures! Did he actually mean—?"

"Over a hundred thousand dollars a year for the rest of my life."

I was staggered. "I could see how that would start to work on you."

"Let me be clear, Dallas, I wasn't totally surprised that a person who might become famous overnight could make a lot of money and even be financially secure, but just for wearing a brand of shoes and making a few personal appearances? I was as stunned as you seem to be."

"Stunned is right."

"Well, the next time someone called from another company, I was feeling very excited and very independent—and very grown up. I said I'd be happy to meet with them but just to listen because I had an agent who would meet with them later. I never should have done that."

"You mean you signed something without Omar?"

"Oh, no! Nothing was offered. Like I say, everything was dependent upon how I did at the olympics, but this one was a million dollar deal, up front, if I won more than one gold medal."

"Wow."

"Dallas, I know it's hard to believe, but I was really not bothered by the money that much."

"I would have been."

30

"I might have been too if I hadn't thought it all through and prayed it all through before. I knew I would be giving a lot of it to God through helping people who needed it, and giving to my church and to missionaries and other Christian endeavors. I knew it would help my coach and my parents, but still—even with that good attitude—meeting with people before I should have was a big mistake."

"I'm not sure I follow you."

"Simply because it took my concentration off my job. And it appeared later to Omar as if I had left him out in the cold. He had to attack something or someone for my bad performance, and when there was no one to blame but me, he blamed me."

"But all that money didn't shake you up?"

"It was fun to dream, but my motivation wasn't for money. It was for the sport, for the competition, and for the Lord. I mean that. I told the Lord that any platform my fame brought me would be used for Him."

"Seems like He would have made it happen just for that reason."

She smiled and sat on the floor.

I did the same.

She cocked her head. "You'd think so, but He doesn't work that way. He doesn't need me or my money or my fame. He just wants obedience."

"Were you disobedient?"

She sat staring straight ahead. "I don't think so. I don't know what happened. I did feel that a lot of people were depending on me and that any little mistake could cost me everything. I was feeling my age, knowing that I would never have another shot like that. And so when I watch the tapes, and I've seen them hundreds of times, I understand why the edge was not there. The risk, the danger, the flair was gone. The routines were perfect, but the personality was missing. I played it safe. Right into oblivion."

"But you went to the olympics."

"Yes, and I supported the other girls and was glad for them when they won, and I pasted on that smile, knowing all the while that it could have been me on that victory stand. I know how terrible that sounds, Dallas, but I mean it when I say I wasn't jealous or envious or self-centered. I was just disappointed that I had not achieved the goal I had set for myself in spite of all the training and work and talent. I had squandered my gifts, and that still bothers me."

"So, then what happened? I mean, how did you happen to move here?"

"Oh, Dallas, I don't know if you have the time to hear what happened when we got back to the United States. That's another story altogether."

"I wouldn't miss it for anything. What time is it?"

"Seven-twenty."

"Tell me the story."

10.00

5

Omar's True Colors

Deborah Lambert sat with her back against the wall as she had when she first stepped off the balance beam. I sat next to her, listening. She told a sad, almost scary story of people she thought were friends, who had turned on her.

"It was the strangest thing, Dallas. At the olympics, I was treated like spoiled meat. It wasn't anything mean or nasty, but none of the girls wanted my advice. They were afraid, I guess, that whatever had happened to me to cause me to lose my place on the team after having done so well was contagious.

"I traveled with them, ate with them, slept in the same room, rode in the same van, dressed in the same locker room, and wore the same uniform. But I was an outsider, a pretender. It was their week, their show, their success. They spoke to me less and less until it was as if I was just part of the furnishings."

"What about Omar Haller?"

She put her hands behind her head and let her head drop back till she was looking at the ceiling. "Omar was the worst of all. He was shameless. Even though I was his only student at the games, and the odds were great against my getting the chance to compete—which I didn't—he came anyway. At his own expense. I offered to help pay his way since I had been responsible for his being there with nothing to do.

"He made it clear to me that he had plenty to do and that he didn't need any of my meager funds. 'I will be recruiting,' he told me, 'so just don't worry about me.' It was embarrassing. Everybody in the world knew he was my coach and that he had all but abandoned me. He tried to pry the other girls away from their coaches, and, when he was unsuccessful at that, he set up secret appointments with girls from other countries, trying to get them to defect."

"He wanted them to move to the United States so he could train them?"

"Exactly. Only he stupidly went after the best in each country, girls who were carefully protected by their governments and who already had all the personal coaching they needed or wanted—and for free. They turned him down flat, reported him, and he got an official reprimand from the International Olympic Committee."

"Did you have any contact with him when you were there?"

"It was impossible to avoid him. He always looked at me with this whipped puppy dog expression, as if to say that he couldn't put into words the pain I had caused him. Finally, near the end, we talked about it. At least he did.

"He said, 'You know why you failed, don't you?'

"I said I didn't consider four scores of nine-eight-five or above failure. He said, 'For someone of your caliber, it was a disaster. It's the end of your career. You're finished. You choked. You didn't have the guts, the character. You got self-centered and took upon yourself all the business negotiations, got your mind off what you were supposed to do, got a taste of what life in the fast lane would be like, and then it scared you to death.'

" 'You couldn't follow my plan. You couldn't wait. And with all the pressure of what one false move could do to your future, your career, your security, you choked. Plain and simple.' "

She sighed and continued. "It was hard to argue with, so I didn't try. Maybe he was right, but what he said next was unfair. 'I knew what you were up to,' he told me. 'You were gonna close me out, stiff me, take my share. You didn't need Omar anymore, now that you had made it on your own. Only you didn't make it, and now you're going to regret trying to do that, because you're going to wind up paying me as if you'd won and signed all those deals.' "

I was puzzled, and I'm sure it showed. "What did he mean by that?"

"I didn't know, and I wouldn't find out until we got back to the States. I was so numbed, so hurt, so disappointed in him, I didn't know what to say. I just ran from him in tears. I was still grieving over my not making the olympic team, and right there in the olympic gym, he lays that horrible charge on me."

"What'd you do?"

She smiled at the thought. "I knew he was going to be there for the evening's competition. Everyone was healthy, eager, and strong, so I knew I wouldn't get to perform. During the warm-ups, I went to the uneven bars. I was still crying, but I don't know that anyone could tell.

"Dallas, I can't explain it, but I felt supercharged. The fans were watching the various teams warm up. Several girls were in line at each apparatus, stretching, bending, chatting, waiting their turn for a few moments on the equipment to get a feel for it or try their dismounts, whatever.

"I was fourth of six girls at the uneven bars. Hardly noticed, I moseyed to the back of the line. When another girl came, I let her go ahead of me. I wanted more time on the bar than anyone else, and I didn't want to make anyone wait. Soon an announcement came in several languages: five minutes till the end of the warm-up period.

"Three of the girls left the uneven bars and joined a mass of athletes on the floor exercise mat. When I was the only one left waiting at the unevens, I tried to appear eager to get in some practice so the girl on the bars would hurry. I was bursting with energy.

"In one of those rare occasions where things work out just so, the other girls were all leaving their apparatus when I mounted the uneven bars. The gym grew quiet, the people idly watched. At first. Then they watched with intensity. And all the other competitors watched too.

"Dallas, I hit it."

"You hit it? You hit what?"

"It's an expression. I hit a perfect routine, better than I had ever dreamed. It was just a personal statement to anyone who cared to watch. To my coach, to my teammates, to the fans, to the other competitors. Everyone knew I was an alternate who had showed well in the world championships two years before and also in the olympic trials earlier this year, but who had failed to make the first team.

"For my first maneuver, people knew they were watching something special. I had such energy I could hardly contain it. I was in my warm-up suit, yet I bounced and whirled and flew in and around and through those bars with power. My dismount was a triple back, which I stuck without a waver, a move I had never even tried in practice before."

I turned to glance at Deborah because she had quite talking. In the faint light I could see a tear rolling down her cheek. Her eyes were full, but she had a faraway look and a slight smile at the memory. Clearly, she was still there. When she spoke again, her whisper was throaty and thick.

"It was a ten, Dallas. The applause proved it. Applause from everywhere, from everyone. Well, maybe not from Omar. I confess I was embarrassed as I joined the team and we filed back into the locker room to prepare for the official procession into the gym. There was pity in the eyes of my teammates.

"A network television official grabbed me just as I was leaving the floor. 'You're Lambert, aren't you?' I nodded. 'U.S. champ?' I had been, but having not made the first team, I just shrugged. 'But you're an alternate?' I nodded again.

38

'Who are you replacing tonight?' My tears told him that I was replacing no one. I pulled away from him and heard him mutter, 'Sure wish we'd got *that* routine on tape!' "

I knew it was past seven-thirty and that my teammates must already be in the equipment room with Stan, getting outfitted. But I wanted to know what had happened when Deborah returned to the States. It hadn't been that many months ago that my family and I had been glued to the television set every night watching the U.S. olympic team. Suddenly our best gymnast, though she didn't compete in the olympics, had moved away from her Texas home, now lived in our state, started attending our church, was coaching in a local gymnastics shop, and was about as removed from international competition as you could get.

I just sat staring at her, not having realized before how fragile she seemed, in spite of her height and her conditioning. She was just a nineteen-year-old girl, after all. I had seen her as a woman, being so much older than I was, but for some reason, nineteen still sounded young to me. She was still a teenager, and I was almost one.

She sniffed and ran her hands through her hair. "I came home to Texas, and it was all over. No one wanted to talk to me, to interview me, to sign me, to have me coach or compete or anything. People at my church didn't know what to say. They had followed me for years, just knowing that someday I would be the olympic champion. Now I was nothing.

"It wasn't just pity on their parts. It was disappointment. I think they saw me as a failure. And maybe I was."

"That's why you moved?"

"Oh, no! I could have survived that, even though it was difficult for my parents to see me go through such pain. It was the lack of any work to do, the feeling of being shut out by all my former friends and teammates. You know, when it's over it's over. But what really iced it was the lawsuit."

"The lawsuit?"

"Omar filed a suit against me."

39

"For what?"

"For breach of an oral contract."

"Which means what?"

"He says we had an agreement, even though it wasn't in writing, that he would be my agent and manager and that he would get a certain percentage of all my earnings for a certain period following the olympics."

"Was it true?"

"Yes."

"So, what does that mean?"

"He goes on to say that I breached the agreement, or broke it, by acting irresponsibly and performing below par, costing him hundreds of thousands of dollars."

"So he takes you to court?"

She nodded. "He sued me for over a million dollars."

"Can he win?"

"He doesn't intend to."

"Now you've really lost me."

6
Caught!

Deborah explained that Omar was almost satisfied by her horror upon learning that she had had a suit filed against her. She had called him and demanded to know what it was all about.

"I thought it would get your attention," he had said.

"It got my attention all right! What am I supposed to do now?"

"You can settle out of court. Either way, you'd better get yourself an attorney."

"Are you serious?"

"You bet I am."

"Omar, after all we've been through together? I make a little mistake, get beat in the olympic trials, and all of a sudden we're not friends anymore."

"We're worse that just not friends anymore, Deborah. You messed with my livelihood. I've coached you at bargain prices for seven years, hoping for the day when I could manage your career and we would both benefit. I'm not going to be left out in the cold."

"Omar, I can't afford an attorney. You know that."

"Then you'd better start thinking about settling out of court."

"How does one do that?"

"We agree on a figure."

"A dollar figure?"

"Exactly."

"How much?"

"You tell me, Deb."

Deborah told me she hated it when anyone called her Deb or Debbie, and that Omar knew that.

"How can I tell you? I don't have any experience extorting money from people who don't have any."

"Well, you'd better start thinking in terms of six figures."

Deborah turned to me. "That time, Dallas, I knew what six figures meant. There was no way I could ever come up with that kind of money—and even more, I wouldn't have come up with it if I was a multi-millionaire. A lawyer in our church told us that the only way Omar could hope to win a case against me would be if he could prove that I had intentionally failed to make the olympic team for the express purpose of defaming him or injuring him financially."

"So what did you tell him?"

"I called his bluff. I told him that I would neither settle out of court nor hire an attorney to represent me in court if he filed."

"I'll bet that stopped him."

"He slammed the phone down. I fully expected to be served with papers within the next few days, but nothing happened. I had almost forgotten about his threats until someone called about ten days later. A man said he was an attorney representing Omar Haller and that he was calling to inform me that the suit had been filed.

"I simply thanked him for calling and didn't ask what I should expect or what I was supposed to do about it. He sounded like a phony to me, and sure enough, when nothing came in the mail a few days later, I passed it off as a threat dreamed up by Omar.

"When Omar himself called to tell me he had put it on hold for a while, I knew he was lying and that whoever had called was not a lawyer but had been put up to it by Omar. 'Let's just settle this between ourselves,' he told me. 'I'm willing to forget it for a lump sum of eighty thousand.'

"Our friend at church had told me how to respond when Omar started negotiating and reducing the price. 'You can say you'll settle for a dime.' I told him, 'and you won't get it from me.' He said, 'Well, then I'm forced to take you to court for the million.' I told him to just do it and quit bothering me.

"A few days later, he called again. The price was down to fifty thousand. 'That doesn't sound like much,' he told me, 'but if I invest it, I can get a regular income from it. I'll be able to live in spite of the fact that I have nothing for all the years I sacrificed to teach you everything I know.'

"I told him, 'Omar, you know I'm a Christian. I tell the truth. I believe in doing what's right. To pretend to believe you would be deceiving. I don't want to be unkind to you either, so just let me be frank. I'm moving out of state. If you want to contact me by mail, just write me at my home church and my legal counsel will forward your message to me. End of conversation. Good-bye.'

"He tried to say something, but I hung up. Part of me wondered whether I would be served papers before I left town, but another part of me knew he was still bluffing. I wasn't trying to run from my problems, but I needed a fresh start. I needed to come somewhere where people appreciated a career that fell just short of olympic gymnastics first team. And I found it here.

"Found a good church too. A good university. A good gymnastics coaching and teaching spot. And a good gym."

"Find any good friends?"

She looked at me and grinned a big grin. Embarrassing me to death, she threw her arm around me and drew me close, tousling my hair. "At least one!" She laughed. I blushed and sat rather stiffly, waiting for her to let me loose.

But before she did, the lights came on, and Stan and my friends saw me sitting there with Deborah Lambert's arm around me!

All of them stood gawking at us, expressionless. She was still laughing. I was dying. Finally, she let go of me, and I bounded to my feet.

She stood slowly, welcoming the guys. "Tonight's get acquainted night! You'll see what it's all about, and within three years, you'll be champions!"

Jimmy muttered. "Champions of what?"

She beamed. "Who knows? Who cares?"

Stan glared at her, his lips pursed. "Truer words were never spoken."

She was leading us to the men's part of the complex. "What do you mean?"

"That tonight's get acquainted night. The kid is twelve years old, Debbie."

She laughed loud. "Deborah to you, Stanley. And you can think what you want. Dallas O'Neil happens to be a full-fledged he-man woman hater. I hugged him because he's my new friend."

It would take me a couple of weeks to live down the razzing I got from that little incident. It was hard to convince the guys that I didn't like it when she threw her arm around me, even before Stan turned on the light.

That had been a memorable night for more than one reason. I had heard quite a story, of course, but the rest of the time was hilarious. If you could have seen all of us inexperienced kids trying to simply mount the various apparatus!

By then all the regular gymnasts had returned for their workouts, and Deborah asked them to show us simple routines, how to mount and dismount, where to put our hands, all that. The equipment that looked the easiest was really the hardest.

The high bar, or horizontal bar, was easy to hang from if someone gave you a boost to get you up there, but after that, most any of us could do was swing from it for a while and drop to the mat.

Jack did a couple of chin-ups, but none of us were ready to pull ourselves through or even get close to attempting a giant swing. That name is a good one for the move, because when Stan jumped up and swung a few times, then did a giant swing, we were thrilled.

He swung all the way over the top. I didn't think I would ever learn to do that, and from the looks on the faces of the others guys, I knew they thought the same thing.

The pommel horse was the worst, but it looked most difficult to start with. It's covered with leather and has two wood handles in the middle. Once you finally hoist yourself up there, it's hard to know what to do next.

The pommel horse expert at the North American Turners' Gym sprang aboard and went through a series of spins and turns, supporting his weight first by one hand and then the other. At one point he drove his legs high in the air, and when he swung back down he had to get each hand out of the way just in time. It was incredible.

Toby got on the horse and swung his legs over to straddle it. He could support his weight on his hands for only so long, and he tried to swing the way he had seen the expert do it. Every time his strength gave out and he crumbled between the wood handles, we laughed till we cried.

The floor exercise was the most fun because there were hardly any rules. Stan explained that in competition there are certain graded movements from one difficulty to the other, and that for the highest possible score, several maneuvers are required.

But after we watched a few people who knew what they were doing move through their routines, we all got on the mat at the same time and took turns clowning around. Deborah had warned me, and I had warned the guys, that we had to behave and not disrupt anything, but even she was enjoying our antics.

It was clear to me that even if we paid the money for the use of the gym and Deborah taught us regularly, it would be many months before any of us would be able to do much of anything on any piece of the men's equipment. The women's stuff looked like more fun, but I knew we wouldn't be any good at that either.

Still, she was willing and had promised to make champions of us if we would apply ourselves. I would have to ask the guys how they liked their first real exposure to the sport and to the coach and see if they wanted to invest the time.

I still wanted to talk to Deborah, but I didn't dare with all the guys there. They were going to be on my case enough with what they had seen, or thought they had seen, earlier. After we all made fools of ourselves on the parallel bars, we headed for the locker room to change back into our street clothes.

We reminded each other to thank Deborah on our way out, and the guys told me I had more to thank her for than they did. I thought about throwing a towel at the next guy who said anything like that, but I had to be an example of good behavior if we were going to start going to the gym regularly.

As we filed out, thanking Deborah and the other gymnasts who had showed us so much, Stan called out to her from the office. "Deborah! Phone for you! Guy by the name of Haller! Omar Haller!"

7

More Trouble for Deborah

Leaving that gym that night was one of the hardest things I've ever done. I wanted to stay, to sit in the room while she talked on the phone—better yet, to find an extension phone and listen in.

Even though she had embarrassed me to death by putting her arm around me in the dark—and I knew she meant nothing but friendship by it—I felt very close to her. She had flattered me by being so honest that she even told me things that made her cry.

The guys, of course, all demanded to know if I was in love. I wasn't. I said so, and I think they knew it. But to some of them, sitting in the dark with a beautiful nineteen-year-old athlete was something to be envied.

For some reason, she treated me like a friend, and she trusted me enough to tell me that whole story. Somehow I didn't want to be left out of it now that this Omar Haller was back in her face again. How did he find her, get her number? What did he want now?

It was something I couldn't discuss with the guys on the way home. She hadn't sworn me to secrecy or even asked me not to tell anyone, but sometimes you just know that some things are secrets.

I made the guys change the subject from what they discovered when Stan turned the light on. "Once and for all, forget that, believe me that it was innocent, and tell me what you want to do about a gymnastics team."

They wanted to know what *I* wanted to do about it. "It's going to take a lot of time and work, Dallas. And we'll probably not be good at it for years. Just like swimming."

"But you guys enjoyed the swimming team."

"We enjoyed the coach, Johnny Cloud. Looks like *you* would enjoy this coach, Dal."

If I'd smiled and laughed off that comment, maybe they would have let up on me, but I was past the point of humor. I was worried about Deborah and her phone call, and I had my mind on that. So the guys kept up the teasing.

Jimmy Calabresi, my best friend, hung around at my place before going home. "Jim, I gotta get serious about this thing. Deborah was nice to us tonight, and she's made us a generous offer. Seriously, where do you think the guys are on it? Do they want to become a team and let her teach and coach us, or not?"

Jimmy stared at me, as if catching on to the question for the first time. "Are you serious?"

"Of course I'm serious! What do you think this evening has been all about?"

"You mean you really don't know how the guys felt about tonight?"

I nodded.

"They loved it. It may wear off, and they may lose interest when they find out how right they are about being afraid it will take a long time to get good. But no, they want to form a team, they want you as captain, and they want Deborah Lambert as coach."

"And what do they think about finding us in the dark, with her arm around me?"

"Her arm was around you? Ho! Dallas!"

"You knew that!"

"I did not! I don't think anybody did. It took our eyes a few seconds to get used to the light, and we couldn't tell what you'd been doing. Nobody thinks you're interested in her as a girl friend, and they *know* she's not interested in you that way."

He said that a little too forcefully. I knew she wasn't interested in me *that way* either, but I didn't want it to seem *that* much out of the question. "So, anyway, I should tell her that we're on, that we want to take her up on her offer?"

Jimmy nodded. "Yeah, and tell her we're all excited about it. We're athletes, and we've had some success, so we're going to want to work hard and get as good as we can as fast as we can in gymnastics."

I used that errand—telling her of our decision—to justify going to the gym the next day after school. She didn't offer any comment about her phone call, but I planned to ask her about it anyway. She started with small talk.

"When do you have to be home for dinner, Dallas?"

"A couple of hours. Why?"

"Just wondering. Wouldn't want to make you late."

"You don't want to talk to me?"

"Sure I do. It's all right."

She was sitting on a table in her sweatsuit. I got the impression that she was treating me differently than she had the evening before. I told her so.

"Why?"

"I don't know. I can just feel it. It's almost as if you wished you hadn't told me as much as you did."

She winced. "You're a very perceptive boy."

"Maybe, but I don't even know what that means."

"It means you understand a lot of things, people in particular."

"I don't understand you. Last night you treated me like one of your oldest friends, and today you seem a little distant to me."

"You hit it right on the head when you said that I wished I hadn't told you so much."

"But why? I can be trusted. I care. I'm going to be around here a lot as the captain of the team you're going to coach."

"Oh."

"Oh? That's all I get for that news? 'Oh'?"

"I'm sorry, Dallas. It's just that I may have to reconsider that."

I shook my head. "This isn't my day. First you act like I'm just any old kid, not the one you spilled your guts to last night, not the one you said was your friend. Then I tell you news that's supposed to thrill you, and I get an *Oh*, and now you tell me you may have to change your plans, as if it's just a matter of having a picnic inside instead of outside on a rainy day. What's going on, Deborah?"

She folded her arms, let her head fall back, closed her eyes, and sighed deeply. "Got time for a walk around the block?"

"That's more like it. But that's a mighty big block."

"Might take us twenty minutes, Dal."

"You're on." She had called me Dal and suggested the walk, so maybe things were going to get back to normal.

The late afternoon was crisp, and the sun was already low in the sky. Deborah grabbed a down-filled jacket and turned up the collar against the wind. I could tell from the color in her cheeks that she had been working out and could easily chill in that weather.

We walked toward the west and squinted against the setting sun. "Well, Dallas, you were right. I went home last night wondering why I had troubled you with so much of my story. You'll remember that two nights ago I tried to weasel out of telling you anything. You mentioned the olympics, and I clammed up, but you insisted.

"I put you off for a night, but sure enough, you showed up early and alone and really seemed to care and to want to know. So I opened up."

"And have I done anything to make you wish you hadn't?"

She shook her head. "It's just me. You're a very bright, very likable boy, Dallas. And I wouldn't want to say anything to hurt you, but you are, after all, still a twelve-year-old boy. It was wrong of me to tell you of the way people can hurt each other, the depths they can go to. I'm sorry, but there's nothing you can do about my problem, so I shouldn't have shared it."

I was trying to think of a good way to answer that and to assure her that I could pray for her, think about her, try to advise her—even if I was "just a kid"—but she changed the subject before I could get it out.

"I was certain that your friends and you were not going to take me up on my offer to coach you. I could see that they had fun, but they had to be frustrated as accomplished athletes to not be able to do anything they saw the experts do. We watch the olympics, and it all looks so effortless, but we've had football players leave the gym in tears after a half hour."

We turned a corner. "Well, they want to start a team and train every other day."

"Oh, I see."

"So now it's 'Oh, I see.' I guess that's an improvement."

She chuckled. "Well, Dallas, I can't hide from you the fact that Omar called me at the gym last night. That complicates everything."

"How did he find you?"

"Huh! He lied to our lawyer friend at my old church. He said he's seen the error of his ways and wanted to let me know personally that he was dropping all threats of legal action. He told my friend that he had just been angry and let his temper get the best of him."

"Are you mad at your friend for giving Omar your number?"

"Nah. I wish he had called for my permission first, but it could have happened to anyone, and I probably would have told him to go ahead and give it anyway. Omar can be very charming, very misleading. Our friend had no reason to mistrust him."

"But that's not what Omar was calling to tell you, was it?"

55

"Well, sort of."

"But there were strings attached."

"Exactly."

I walked on a few steps before realizing that she had stopped and was just staring at me with her hands on her hips. I looked up at her. "Sometimes you do seem a lot older than you are, Dallas. I may wind up glad that I have confided in you."

"Just don't stop now. I want to know what Omar said."

She caught up with me, and we continued walking. "Well, he said just what my lawyer friend said he would say, but with—"

"Strings, like I said."

"Right. He said he would drop all the threats, call off the lawyers, stop pressuring me to try to get me to settle out of court, forgive me, and—get this—start over."

"Start over?"

"Start over. That's what he said."

"Deborah, he didn't mean—"

She nodded. "That's exactly what he meant. He wanted to become my coach, agent, and manager again."

"Of course you told him to forget it."

"That's what my head told me to do."

"But you didn't?"

She seemed embarrassed to have to shake her head. "I'm a Christian, Dallas. So are you. Am I not supposed to forgive someone who apologizes and wants to start over?"

8

A New Twist

Now, there was a question and a half. How was I supposed to answer that one? It sounded good. Logical. Fair. But something was wrong.

Did I have the right, as a twelve-year-old talking to an almost-twenty-year-old to try to set her straight? I began cautiously as we made a turn that put us back on the same street as the gym, a long block away.

"Deborah, I have two questions about this and about this guy. First, can you believe him? I mean, he pestered your lawyer friend into giving him your number. And then he added the condition that you accept him back as your coach and everything. Do you have to treat him like anyone else who asks for forgiveness? Forgiveness can't be bought or forced, and dropping threats against someone can't come with conditions."

She appeared deep in thought. "Like I've said before, Dallas, you sometimes seem older than you are. I *have* felt a little funny about being the guilty one in this whole thing. It wasn't my fault that he felt the way he did, and I have admitted and apologized for talking with business people and for performing below par. And you're right, this still puts him in the driver's seat."

"He still wants something from you."

"Oh, he sure does. He wants more than ever from me now. He said he had coached me at bargain rates for years, but it's just not true. I talked to other girls, skaters, gymnasts, and others, and what my parents paid him was pretty much the same other coaches were getting. Some of the big names got more, of course, and many received less. I can't feel bad about what we paid him. For one thing, it was what he asked for."

"So, what would he charge you now?"

"Nothing. Just fifteen percent of everything I earn because of how I do."

"That leads me to my second question, Deborah."

"Yeah, you said you had two."

"I don't want to offend you."

"You won't, Dallas."

"Well, if I do, I won't mean to."

"I know. Go ahead."

"Well, I was just wondering what more there is for you to do. You told me yourself that at your age—you're not that old to me, you know—you're kind of, well, uh, old, uh, for, you know, gymnastics."

She laughed. "I know, I know. Go on."

"Well, if the olympics was your last shot, what does Omar Haller want you to do next? Is there a professional gymnastics circuit, or would you be doing movies, television, what? You didn't win a gold at the olympics. In fact, you didn't even compete. Except for those few people who really follow women's gymnastics when the olympics aren't on, no one knows who you are, right?"

She shrugged. "I guess. I was the women's all-around national champion the last two years."

"I hadn't heard of you, and I'm a sports nut."

"Don't rub it in."

"See, I offended you, Deborah, and I didn't mean—"

"You didn't offend me, Dallas. I was just kidding."

"Well, anyway, you've been talking like you're over the hill and that your career is over, yet you work out everyday. Is that just to keep in shape?"

"Yes, that and to be able to show my students how it's supposed to be done."

"C'mon, you're training for something."

She grew so quiet so quickly that I knew I had hit upon something. I just didn't know what. "Whatever it is, it's what Omar Haller wants to train you for."

She said something so softly that I missed it completely. All I knew was that she had spoken. I pretended to have heard. "Oh, is that right?"

She looked at me quickly, and I couldn't keep from smiling. She knew then that I hadn't heard what she had muttered. "I was just saying that I was working out so hard so that I could do it. I could succeed without Omar."

"But for what. The olympics in three and a half years?"

She shook her head. "I could never complete with the kids. I've told you that."

"Sorry."

"I wasn't scolding you, Dallas. I just haven't told anyone what I'm training for, and to tell you the truth, the last thing in the world I want is to have anything more to do with Omar."

"That's easy. Tell him no. Tell him off. Tell him he's forgiven, but that you're through with him. Then get on with working out for whatever it is you're planning for, and be sure to invite me."

"To Frankfurt? How would you get there?"

"Frankfurt, Kentucky?"

"No, that's Frankfort. I'm talking Frankfurt, West Germany."

"The world games?"

"You turkey! You *do* follow all sports!"

"It just came to me."

"Promise you won't tell anyone, Dallas."

"I promise, but forget worrying about how *I* would get there. How would *you* get there? Who would sponsor you?

61

The U.S.?"

"They'd sort of have to. I'm the defending national champion. If I won the national championship again this year, they have to send me to Frankfurt next year."

"But you're not too old, like you've been saying?"

"Of course I am. But, Dallas, I have never been so determined about anything in my life. I'm going to qualify anyway."

"Why don't you just go for a third straight national all-around championship and call it quits?"

"What would that prove? That I should have made the olympic team? Everyone knows that. It would just bring up the old question of why or how I choked and whether I could handle the tougher, international competition."

"But if you went on to win the world championship, you would have made up for that failure."

"Exactly. And it's what I want to do."

"And no one else knows?"

"No one."

"Just me?"

"Just you."

"And your parents."

"Just you, Dallas. No one else knows. Not Stan, none of my students, not even my parents."

"But why?"

"I work better that way. With private goals."

"I won't tell anyone."

"You just can't, Dallas. I want to go at this with such a singleness of purpose that I can't fail. And I'm confident that God is in it."

"What makes you think so?"

"Because I've prayed it through, and I do everyday."

"But how will you know He's heard you? When you win it all?"

"No. I don't have to win. I want to, and I believe I will, but I'm doing it for entirely different motives than before. I want to show people that I haven't squandered my gift and that I should have been an olmypic champion, but I won't be doing it for myself."

"Then what will you do with all the money that you'll get after it happens?"

"That's just it. My goal is not to become a commercial person, an actress, a 'famous' type. I want to get married someday, have a home and family and be active in a church. Great amounts of money would distract me, turn my head the way just thinking about them did last time."

"Then you'll give all the money to God? Like to churches and missionaries and stuff like that?"

She shook her head. "No. As I said, I've prayed it through, Dallas. I've meditated on Scripture while thinking about it too. You know what God showed me? That He doesn't need my money. He doesn't need the world's money. He doesn't need the devil's money. What He wants, what He longs for, what He'd love to have is people, us, you and me. I take that message personally."

We were back at the gym. Deborah sat on the steps outside, and I sat next to her. All of a sudden I didn't care who saw me sitting there. She was a wonderful friend, and she trusted me with secrets, and she was teaching me things. I felt good about her. I was still a he-man woman hater, at least as far as girls my own age went, and as far as love and kissing and marriage and all that went. But I liked Deborah Lambert, and I didn't mind being seen with her. I would have traded a lot of teasing from my friends for the lesson I had just learned. But, of course, I was still puzzled.

"So, you win the nationals for the third time in a row. You represent the U.S. with the rest of the team at the world's, and you're the darkhorse favorite because you've shown well there before but were only an alternate at the olympics.

"You win that too and become the talk of international gymnastics. You're a star because everybody watches it on TV and reads about you in newspapers and magazines. The same people who wanted to talk to you before the olympic trials make you offers even better than you would have gotten then.

"So, what are you going to to with the millions?"

She leaned forward and stared into my eyes. "You don't get it, do you?"

I felt hurt. I had figured out most of the rest of it. She could have given me credit for that. My pain showed. "What?"

She reached out and squeezed my shoulder to let me know she was still being friendly, even though she was jabbing me for not catching her whole point. "I'll use the platform for God, just as I would have before. Only this time, there will be nothing cluttering the message."

"I still don't know what you'd do with the money."

She cocked her head and smiled. "I'd turn it down, Dallas. I'd turn down every cent. I don't need it. I don't want it. God doesn't need it or want it. It would only be distracting."

"That'll sure get people's attention."

"I hope so. Then I can focus that attention on Him."

It was a wonderful thought, a great plan. That's why I was surprised when Deborah looked past me, over my shoulder, and the color seemed to drain from her face.

9
Omar

I turned just in time to see a tall, leggy man in his early forties step from a sleek, late model sports car. He wore tight jeans, slip-on shoes, a furry jacket, and a leather cap. "Deb, darling!"

She stood, her hands still in her pockets. I sat right where I was. "Hello, Omar. I wasn't expecting you, and I have some coaching to do in a few minutes."

"Cancel it. We have to talk." He looked down at me with a phony smile. "Get lost, kid, huh?"

I don't know where I got the boldness. Maybe it rubbed off from Deborah. I stared right into his eyes but directed my question at her. "How could you stand this for seven years? Was he always this way?"

"I was too young. His true colors didn't come out until recently. He was always an ornery coach. I knew better, but my parents thought that was an act to bring out the best in me."

He reached for her, still smiling. "It was, Deb. Now get rid of the brat, will you? Let him go tell your boss that you're not working tonight. You're going out to dinner with your coach and agent."

"I can get out of the coaching myself, Omar. But the kid stays right where he is for as long as he wants to. And so do I.

I'm not going anywhere with you. If you're rude enough to drop in unannounced, you'll have to talk to me right here, on my terms. Fair enough?"

I was so proud of her, and of the fact that she wanted me to stay, I could have burst.

She turned and jogged up the steps. "I'll be right back." And she was gone. Now *that* was embarrassing, but clearly as much for Omar as for me.

"You're a student of hers, eh, kid?"

It was true, but less true than what I told him. "I'm her friend. We go to the same church."

He nodded knowingly. "Ah." It carried a lot of meaning. We found it hard to look at each other. "I s'pose she told you of my plans for her."

I shook my head as if I wasn't interested anyway. She hadn't told me. In fact, I don't think *he* had told *her*. He probably had only the nationals in mind, not the worlds like she did. I wasn't going to give away one of her secrets. He was slick, though.

"We've been together a lot of years. I'm gonna take her to the top. We're gonna make each other a lot of money."

I couldn't resist. "You're going to make *her* money?"

"I made her what she is today." He sat on a step. "Yeah, taught her gymnastics, everything. It's payday now."

"You weren't paid before?"

"Sure, but that was chickenfeed compared to what we're going to knock down now, kid."

"My name's, Dallas."

"You from here? I have my training center in San Antonio."

I shook my head as if I couldn't have cared less. And I couldn't have. I was trying to work up some compassion or at least some sympathy for this guy. I had to hand him one thing: he was honest about his greed. He might not have been honest in all his dealings, but he was up front about that.

Deborah returned. "You two get acquainted?"

"Yeah, this kid, uh, Dallas and I are buddies already. He's

all right."

I piped up. "He's going to make you rich, Deborah."

She laughed. "No one's going to make me rich."

"Yes, I am, Deb. Now you want to talk in private or not?"

"I already told you. My evening is free, but it's going to start and end right here. Got it?"

"You're kinda uppity for a little girl I started teaching when she was twelve."

"Don't remind me."

That sounded pretty cold, and I looked quickly at her. "I didn't mean to say it that way, Omar. It's just that we were together alot of years. They were all right, they were good. We never got along terribly well, but you knew your stuff. And I'm not twelve anymore, Omar. In case you missed it, I've grown up."

"Not as much as you think, girl."

"What's that supposed to mean?"

"Just what it sounds like. You're the one who blew the deal at the trials. Do we have to go into it all again?"

"Please, let's not. Let's put it behind us. It didn't turn out the way we wanted it to, and I take the blame. Are you going to forgive me? I've forgiven you for abandoning me at the olympics and for threatening to sue me over it."

"You know I'll forgive you, Deb. But I want something in return."

I couldn't hold back. "That's not forgiveness; that's blackmail."

Omar glared at me, but I was really hurt when Deborah put a finger to her lips. I wanted to apologize all over myself, but I felt so bad I couldn't say anything. Me and my big mouth. I decided to stay out of it from then on, and I almost did. She made me feel a little better with her next comment, though.

"He's right, you know."

"Oh, great. Real religious girl. Won't even forgive a guy."

"Omar, you've always thrown my faith up in my face. It was my faith that allowed me to forgive you. I mean it, and it

69

comes with no strings attached. If your forgiveness depends on some conditions, then I'm going to have to just go without it."

"You don't really have a choice."

"I have to accept your forgiveness *and* your conditions?"

"That's right."

"Don't push me, Omar."

The sun was completely gone now. Omar stood and walked a couple of steps away, then turned to face her. The light from a streetlamp shone behind him. His voice came in a whine. "Deb, we had a good thing going."

"If we had such a good thing going, why do you call me by a name you know I don't like?"

"I'm sorry, Deborah." He was sarcastic now. "We had a little falling out. So let's get on with life. Let me get you into shape for the nationals and see if you can place in that again."

"Place!"

"C'mon! You're not going to win it again with your younger olympic teammates coming back with tons of confidence. Just shoot for placing, winning some kind of medal, even a bronze, and I'll see what kind of deals I can swing for you.

"As the grand old lady of your sport, maybe I can get you some color commentary work on television. Then when you're known to millions of households, we can get a few endorsements. Nothing like if you had won the olympic gold, but not a total loss anyway."

"I count it all but dung." Deborah had said it so quietly, Omar had to lean close to hear her.

"Dung? Is that what you said? Are you calling me that?"

"I'm calling your plan that. TV work, endorsements, money. I'm not motivated by it. I'm sorry."

"Well, *I* am, and you owe me that! Your brilliance in the trials cost me hundreds of thousands of dollars. I'm willing to forgive that if you'll try to keep yourself in good enough shape to get us at least something for all our work."

Deborah stared at him as if she couldn't believe what she had heard. Her eyes filled. "Now you've insulted me. I suppose I shouldn't care."

I thought Omar would do whatever he had to do to keep her tears from falling. I would have. But he was angry. "*I've* insulted *you?!* You've ruined my life! Now we're going to turn this thing around, young lady, or you're going to regret it."

Her tears were flowing freely now. She tried to speak, but couldn't. I pleaded with my eyes for her permission to tell him. She nodded. "Mr. Haller, Deborah is not going to turn her thing around for you, as you say."

"Let her speak for herself."

"No, I'm speaking for her. You make her feel like dirt until she can't talk, so listen to me." My knees were shaking. "She doesn't feel she owes you anything except appreciation for what you taught her and the money her parents paid you over the years for your work."

"Chickenfeed! What do you know about it?"

"I know enough to be sure it wasn't chickenfeed. Both of her parents and she had to work to pay you, and most other athletes wouldn't have taken the time or trouble to do both. And what she paid you was right in line with what other coaches were getting."

Omar looked from me to her and back again. "You told this little jerk what I was paid?"

She shook her head. "And don't call him names. He's a bigger man than you'll ever be."

Omar shook his head as if he couldn't be more disgusted. "Can you talk now, Debbie, or is your little lawyer here still handling that for you?"

I stood, my heart racing. "The reason she couldn't turn anything around for you, Mr. Haller, is that even if she became known as the best gymnast in the whole world—"

"That'll be the day."

"Let me finish. Even if she did, she is not interested in the money, and she wouldn't take any of it. No TV, no commer-

71

cials, no money."

He looked at her. "He's joking."

She shook her head. "My sentiments exactly."

"You're crazy!"

"Thank you."

"What's that supposed to mean?"

She nearly smiled. "I'm a fool for Christ."

"You sure are if you'd let money like that slip through your fingers."

"I'd count it all but loss. Dung."

"You *are* nuts."

"Maybe I am. Why would you want to have anything to do with a crazy lady?"

He just stood staring at us in the darkness. "One final offer, Deborah. I'm pleading with you. I'll respect your religion and all that. I won't hold any grudges. I'll forgive you for the stunt you pulled in the trials. But you let me coach you to the nationals one more time, and let me see what kind of deals I can make for us."

She stood. "The answer is no, Omar. Once and for all. No."

He spun in a circle, as if he couldn't think of anything to say. He pulled an envelope from his pocket and handed it to her in a grand, formal way. Bowing, he spoke. "Then try this on for size."

And he headed back to his car.

10

The Document

Deborah stood there on the steps, the business size envelope in her hands, watching Omar Haller's car pull away. He honked and waved. We ignored him.

She turned to step inside the front door where a light hung from the ceiling in the lobby. I was at her elbow as she tore open the envelope.

With the envelope in one hand and the document in the other, she sighed and let her hands drop to her sides. "Well, he's done it. He's filed. It's official now. I'm being sued for over a million dollars."

I didn't know what to say or do. I didn't know anything about law suits and lawyers and court and all that. I figured she would have to hire her own lawyer, and I asked her if she had enough money.

She shook her head but not to say no. It was more as if she just didn't want to talk about it. She was staring into the distance, the wheels of her mind turning. "I'm not going to defend myself. I'm not going to hire a lawyer. If I'm called to court, I'll just show up and insist that Omar and his lawyer prove that I owe him anything or that I did anything on purpose to cause him harm. The only thing I'll have with me is the total of what we paid him over the last seven-and-a-half-years."

That sounded like a good idea to me, but I didn't say so. I just stood there, wishing there was something I could say or do to make things easier for her. The more I watched her, the more I realized how angry she was becoming. Her face flushed, her hands were clenched. "It's the end of my career, I'll tell you that."

She had said that with such force and conviction that, even though I wanted to argue with her and tell her never to say that, I knew it was better to simply say nothing. "Would you tell the sports club that I will not be coaching them, at least not now? Maybe someday, when this blows over. I'm quitting gymnastics as of right now."

I was thinking, *Oh, please don't!* but I said nothing. I knew she was reacting in anger and, I hoped, saying things she didn't mean and wouldn't follow through on. But she sure sounded like she meant it.

She stood with her back to me, and I wanted her to turn and face me, to let me know she knew I was still there and that I was still with her, backing her, supporting her. But I felt like an intruder. After a long time of silence I muttered a good-bye. "Guess I'd better be goin' now."

"Yeah."

She started up the stairs without looking back, and I felt bad. I knew she was hurting and that there was nothing I could do, but I was feeling left out. I had been part of this for a few days already. She had confided in me. Now, when things seemed at their worst, we both knew I had nothing to offer.

I turned to leave, but I was slow going through the door, hoping against hope that she would turn and say something, anything. A word of thanks, a good-bye, a "keep in touch."

But there was nothing. I felt a strange sensation. I was almost mad at her. For some reason, it seemed nearly selfish of her to not realize that I was hurting too. Maybe she didn't think I understood. And maybe she was right.

But maybe she wasn't too. I understood more than she gave

me credit for. Even though I didn't follow all the technical details of the law, I knew enough to see basically what was happening to her.

All the way home I sulked, trying to keep from hating Omar and knowing that I should pray for him. Pray for Omar? I knew it was what the Bible said we should do for our enemies, but it seemed the farthest thing from what I really wanted to do.

What I would really have enjoyed, I had to admit, was slashing his tires or breaking out his car windows. Those thoughts almost made me laugh, because they were as far from my style as praying for my enemies seemed just then. But maybe that was why my silly mind even thought of it.

Praying for Omar was certainly no more ludicrous than taking the law into my own hands and doing something illegal. And so I tried it. I tried praying for Omar. It wasn't easy, and I hardly knew where to begin or what to say, but I just told God that.

I wanted to pray for Deborah too, especially after all she had taught me that evening. Her idea of not wanting or needing or even accepting any of the money for what she might accomplish would make her, I knew, more popular than any athlete for a long time.

Everyone would want to know why she made the decision, and she would have all kinds of opportunities to tell them about God. She just had to stick with it, to stay in training, to make the nationals and then the worlds. It was more important than ever.

But I couldn't blame her for her first decision to just give it all up. It seemed selfish, sure, but when you've devoted more than a third of your life to something and it turns out as bad as her career had, maybe it seemed like the best thing to do would be to just give it up.

When I got home, I didn't feel like talking about Deborah or her problem. My mother asked me how it went at the gym, and I said it was OK. She asked me if I worked out, and I said no.

"Have you eaten?"

I shook my head.

"You must be hungry, Dal."

I shook it again.

"Let me fix you something."

"Nah. Thanks."

"You have to eat, honey."

"Maybe later. If I want something, I'll make some toast."

She said that was all right, but she had that concerned look. I went up to my room. The phone rang. She hollered up the stairs, "Dallas! It's for you. Deborah Lambert!"

I ran down the hall to the phone in the corner. "Got it, Mom!" Only when I heard her hang up did I say anything.

"Hi, Deborah. It's Dallas."

It was clear she had been crying. "Dallas, I just wanted to apologize."

"You don't have to—"

"Please let me. You have been so sweet, and I want you to know that you are very special to me. I'm glad you were there tonight. You made me brave enough to say what I had to say to Omar."

"You were great, Deborah."

"Yeah, well, maybe. I didn't feel so great, and it seems like it's all falling apart now with this suit, but I felt bad when I realized you had left and I hadn't thanked you. At first I wished I hadn't told you so much, but now I'm glad I have. I needed someone to share this with, and I'm glad it was you."

"Me too."

"I still feel like I never want to see the inside of a gym again, and I feel peace about giving up the sport."

"Do me a favor, will you, Deborah?"

"Anything."

"You mean that?"

"Of course."

"Put off thinking about what you're going to do about gymnastics, at least until tomorrow."

"I won't feel any differently—"

"You never know. Especially because I'm going to be praying for you."

"You are?"

"Yup. I prayed for Omar already."

"Oh!" She sounded surprised, almost startled. "Did you really?"

"It wasn't easy."

"But you actually did that, Dallas?"

"Uh-huh."

"I know I should do that too. You're an example to me, Dallas. I'm proud of you."

"Maybe if you pray for Omar, you'll change your mind about giving up gymnastics."

She didn't respond to that. "Maybe if you pray for me, Dallas, I'll feel even better about giving up the sport."

"That's not what I'll be praying for. Your idea of how to best serve the Lord in it was one of the best I've ever heard. Anyway, why do you need to feel better about your decision? I thought you said you felt peace about it."

"Hm. You got me. I guess what I feel is determined. I just can't see going through all that work when things turn out this way."

"You're angry."

"You bet I am."

" 'Be angry and sin not.' " I chuckled. "I don't even remember where I read that."

"New Testament, kid. You're a regular chaplain. Quit quoting verses to me, will ya? You're going to get to me yet."

"You got that right. Now will you do me the favor of sleeping on your decision? There's nothing you can do about Omar and the suit except, like you say, showing up to tell your side. Meanwhile, you can stay in shape, just in case you win."

"Thanks again, Dallas. Feel free to call me tomorrow, but not too early."

The next morning, before I even had a chance to think

about it, Deborah called me. "Just something quick, Dal. I feel pretty solid about my decision, and I knew it was only fair to share it with you. This is it: until Omar drops the suit, I'm out of gymnastics. And Dallas, I *am* finding myself able to pray for him."

I didn't know what to think of that. I understood it, I guess. But I didn't like it. It didn't seem to make sense that this guy who had taught her the sport and was obviously a gymnastics fan himself could be so mean and unreasonable that he would keep her from realizing her dream.

I called the gym, just on a hunch. "Stan, has a guy been hanging around there by the name of Omar Haller?"

"Yeah, matter of fact he has. Says he's an old friend of Deborah's. I been lettin' him work out. He's got his own gear, and he ain't bad, 'specially on the floor ex. Why? You wanna talk to him?"

"No, just tell him a friend called and will be down to see him this afternoon. Don't tell him it's me. Let him think it's Deborah. Can I trust you, Stan?"

"Can you trust me? Hey, man, any friend of Deborah's is a friend of mine, hear?"

11

Having It Out with Omar

I prayed all day, wondering how I had got myself into this and what in the world I was going to say to the man. I got there early, hoping that he had left and would come back later. I was lucky.

Stan said Omar had immediately assumed that the "friend" was Deborah and that she was going to have good news for him. I told him that, when Omar arrived, to tell him that his friend was waiting in the women's gym.

I waited in there in the darkness, praying some more, sitting with my back up against the same wall where Deborah and I had sat together so recently. Not long after, I heard whistling in the hall and the door opening. Omar entered to find me sitting there, arms wrapped around my knees, looking up at him expectantly.

He looked annoyed. "Where is she?"

"Where is who?"

"Don't toy with me, kid. She didn't say you would be here too."

"She doesn't know I'm here, Omar."

He stopped short and sighed an irritated sigh. "So you're the friend?"

"That's up to you. I'd like to think so."

He shook his head slowly and approached cautiously, as if

he had no choice. "All right. What's going on? What's up?"

"I just wanted to talk to you. Deborah really doesn't know anything about this."

He pressed his lips together and sat on the floor Indian style about six feet from me. He still looked bored. With a deep breath, he told me to get on with it.

I was nervous, but I had to go through with it. "You've really messed up Deborah's life, and now I'm afraid you're the only one who can fix it."

He flinched. "*I* messed up *her* life? I'm the best thing that ever happened to her."

"Just let me finish, OK? This is not easy for me, and you can take it or leave it. You can get up and walk out of here any time you want and do whatever you want with what I tell you, so just let me get it out, all right?"

He raised his eyebrows as if to agree, so I started in. "She told me about you and about how, as a local Y gymnastics instructor and elementary school teacher, you were so enthusiastic about gymnastics.

"The little girls loved you and wanted you to be their coach, but few of them were good enough and hardly any of them could afford to actually hire you and pay you enough to leave your other jobs.

"But Deborah was. You encouraged her, drove her, talked her up, discussed her future with her parents. After she saw the olympics on television at age eleven, her life was changed. It was all she cared about, all she talked about.

"Her parents talked it over and met with you privately. The deal was made. You would train others in your little gymnastics center, but she would be your full-time student. You were tough, demanding, impatient like never before, but then you had given up the other secure things in your life. This had to work. You would have had nowhere else to turn.

"And it worked. Deborah became better than even you ever dreamed she would be. She gave you all the credit, and you centered all your dreams and your future in her. At some point, when she started doing well in national junior competition, you decided she was your ticket to big money and fame."

I paused to see if I was having any effect. Omar was staring at the floor, nodding slightly, no expression. I decided to skip much of the rest of what I had planned to say and get right to the point.

"She's hurting, Omar. The little girl who isn't so little anymore has been crushed by the man who made her the gymnast she is today. Only today she's no longer a gymnast. She's quit the sport, never wants to have anything more to do with it."

He looked up quickly at me, searching my face for any hint of a lie.

I stared him down. "It's over, Omar. She's had it. She's not going to hire a lawyer. She's just going to take whatever you dish out. And if she loses in court, she'll just have to pay whatever she can pay."

"She has no money." He had said it simply, as a fact.

"Of course she doesn't. How could she?"

"She can't quit the sport. She's the only woman her age who can still compete internationally. She's like the fine Russian treasures of the seventies. She's another Ludmilla." He was talking softly, vacantly, as if to himself. "She proved she was still the best in the world during the warm-ups at the olympic finals. She's still got it. All I wanted was a piece of the action. To intimidate her a little. No way I want her to quit the sport."

I decided not to answer. I wanted to just let his last sentence echo through the room and through his mind without interference. He spoke just above a whisper. "I would never really take her into court. Doesn't she know that?"

I shook my head. "No, she doesn't. How could she know that? If nothing else, she believes what you say. You've had control over much of her life for more than seven years."

He hung his head. "Where can I find her?"

85

"She doesn't want to see you, and she's not coming back here."

"I need to talk to her."

"There's nothing she wants to hear from you."

"Not even that I'm dropping the suit?"

"She's heard that before. She thought it was over."

He pulled a scrap of paper from his wallet and scribbled on it with a pen. "This is a full release. She'll know what that means. Tell her she's free of me, totally. She can do what she wants."

"No strings attached?"

"Only one. She can't give up the sport. She must not. If she does, I'll hound her until *she* sues *me*."

We sat in embarrassed silence for a few minutes with not much more to say and yet feeling awkward about leaving. "Deborah and I have been praying for you, Omar."

He turned away and scratched his ear. "You have, huh?"

"She cares a lot about you."

He shrugged. "Well, I just hope my note makes up for some of the pain I caused her. I hope she knows I was just being selfish and that I'm not really that bad a guy."

Over the next six months, Deborah Lambert continued working at the North American Turners' Gym, coaching, teaching, instructing. Her pupils included the Baker Street Sports Club, the craziest bunch of awkward gymnasts you ever saw. I think we gave her more reasons to laugh than anyone.

We climbed around the apparatus like it was monkey bars. She advised that we work in the weight training room to build up our strength. By the end of the six months, we could all mount and dismount each piece of equipment and do a few simple moves. We were a long way from competition.

But also during that time, Deborah worked as she never had before on her own conditioning and routines. I watched her often, and she clearly got better and better. "I have to. The competition is not sitting still either."

Without a personal coach, she qualified for the nationals by winning some state and regional meets by such huge margins that they were no contests. The national finals were held a couple of hundred miles from our home, and my parents let me ride to them with the Lambert family.

What a thrill to see her perform before a live audience! It was obvious she was tight and nervous, but except for a few slight breaks in a couple of routines, she was in the high nines on all her scores.

She finished first in two events, second in two others, and second overall. She sat in the car on the way home, happy and refreshed and only a little disappointed. "You sure learn the difference between first and second when you lose by a few hundredths of a point and then don't get interviewed. I was hoping to be able to say something nice about Omar on TV. This tape will be shown a week from today on a national network."

At home a telegram awaited her. It was from Omar. She read it, sort of smiling but sort of teary too. "He congratulates me, but he also has a couple of hints. Tuck the chin before this move, curl the wrist earlier before that move. He's probably right. I'll have to watch the tape."

The next weekend she watched the meet on TV at our house, his telegram in hand. "He's right. He's right." She kept saying it.

Four months later, at the world championships in Frankfurt, West Germany, broadcast live to the United States, Deborah was a member of the U.S. team. She followed Omar's advice. First, first, second, first, two perfect tens, nothing lower than a nine-nine, and first overall.

Deborah was the world's best all-around woman gymnast. I was crying. So was she. My family crowded close to the television set as she was interviewed. "First I want to thank God, who does all things well. I want to thank my parents who have supported me all these years. And I want to thank my former personal coach, Omar Haller, of San Antonio,

87

Texas, who still keeps in touch occasionally, and without whom I could not have performed so well today."

"What are your plans now, Deborah? Looking forward to the olympics?"

"No, I'm retiring."

"Really? Are you sure?"

"My mind is made up. I'll teach and coach, maybe go back to college."

"No more competition, and that's final?"

"It's final."

"Endorsements? Speaking? Color commentary?"

"I really have no interest in that. I'm looking forward to becoming a private citizen again and enjoying all the things that go along with that."

Over the next several months, every sports magazine and sports section carried articles and editorials about this refreshing new breed of athlete who didn't cash in on her success. Some said she was crazy. Most said she was a breath of fresh air.

I was just proud to say she was my friend.